Dispatches From The Village

Christopher Munyaradzi Mabeza

Langaa Research & Publishing CIG
Mankon, Bamenda

Publisher
Langaa RPCIG
Langaa Research & Publishing Common Initiative Group
P.O. Box 902 Mankon
Bamenda
North West Region
Cameroon
Langaagrp@gmail.com
www.langaa-rpcig.net

Distributed in and outside N. America by African Books Collective
orders@africanbookscollective.com
www.africanbookscollective.com

ISBN-10: 9956-550-88-4

ISBN-13: 978-9956-550-88-3

Dedication

This book is dedicated to the memory of my late uncles,
Aaron Mabeza and Samson Mabeza,
men who were ennobled by real generosity.

Table of Contents

Acknowledgements

Special thanks are due to Prof Francis Nyamnjoh of the University of Cape Town for his inspirational role. His intellectual restlessness has spurred me to continuously try to comprehend the knottiness of the world.

Kudos to my loving parents, Andrew and Miriam Mabeza, for teaching me to empathise with others. I have since learned that before I judge someone, in the words of famed Pulitzer Prize winner, the late Harper Lee, I have to "climb into their skin and walk around in it". My son Taku also deserves special mention for encouraging me to take deep dives into technological sorcery, advice that has helped me to cut on my expenditure on IT wizards. I am increasingly becoming more at home as I beaver away in the new brave new world of IT.

Finally, I will remain eternally grateful to my loving God for helping me scale the academic ladder.

1
An elegiac lament for a bygone era

During my days in the Eastern Cape of South Africa, my favourite pastime was visiting the beach. One day as I drove to Port Alfred from Grahamstown, I could not resist seeking refuge in the rear-view mirror, as I relived my days as a youngster. I started playing a CD of chart busters during my days in the village. The first song I played was *Tsvimbo dzemoto* (Fire arms) by the legendary Zimbabwean band, the Bhundu Boys. The lyrics are as follows:

Tsvimbodzemoto (Fire arms)
Makarekare paruzevha painakidza
Time immemorial life in the rural areas used to be a delight
Makarekare paruzevha painakidza
Time immemorial life in the rural areas used to be a delight
Vanakomana navanasikana vaitamba chinungu
Boys and girls (youngsters) played *chinungu*
Vanakomana navanasikana vaitamba chinungu
Boys and girls (youngsters) played *chinungu*
Vanasekuru nana mbuya vairidze mbira
The elderly (grandfathers and grandmothers) played mbira
Vanasekuru nanambuy avairidze ngoma
The elderly (grandfathers and grandmothers) played mbira
Gare-gare kwakazouya tsvimbodzemoto
Later-on fire arms were introduced
Gare-gare kwakazouya tsvimbodzemoto
Later-on fire arms were introduced
Pakaputika tsvimbodzemoto mafaro ndokupera
The explosion of firearms marked the end of joy

Pakaputika tsvimbodzemoto mafaro ndokupera

The explosion of firearms marked the end of joy

Vanasekuru nana mbuya ndokutizamisha

The elderly (grandfathers and grandmothers) deserted their homes

Vanakomana navanasikana ndokutizamisha

Youngsters (boys and girls) deserted their homes

Vainosangana kudhorobha kwavaikurukura nhamo dzavaiona kumusha panguvayehondo

They reunited in the cities where they narrated the suffering they endured back home during the liberation war

Vainosangana kudhorobha kwavaikurukura nhamo dzavaiona kumushapa nguvayehondo

They met in the cities where they narrated the suffering they endured back home during the liberation war

Listening to the song evoked memories of a bygone era, an era which sadly will never come back, and an era when life in the village was seemingly harmonious. We have to hark back to the days when there was collective responsibility for the infirm, old and poor in the village. For us in the village there was no such a thing as the extended family. We were all one. Family closeness or *esprit de corps* was pivotal in maintaining harmony in the village.

Christmas was such an important time in the village. It was a wonderfully celebratory event. It was time for family reunions. It was quality family time. Family members based in the urban areas would come back home. Brothers and sisters from the urban areas would come back to the village for the Christmas festivities. Showcasing our sartorial muscles was something my siblings and I looked forward to at Christmas. It seems there was a low intensity competition between us and our cousins with regards our outfits at Christmas. My father had an account with one of the leading departmental stores in Gweru, a city about 50km from our village. He was very well conversant with the fashion trends of the day. Therefore, we were well catered for in that department. Often, we came up tops. But at times our cousins from the urban areas thumped us. They left no stone unturned in their bid to impress. I remember one year when their hairdresser made them look strange in the village. To most of us in the village, their hairdos – permed peroxide hair - were weird for boys. The village was humming with the news of their strange hairstyles. But for my cousins, it was show time, marking the beginning of what they proclaimed to be their dominance in the village, fashion-wise. They would tell anyone who cared to listen about how much money they had spent in the hair salon.

Meanwhile, we only got to see our clothes on Christmas day. Our parents told us that Santa Claus came during the dead of night and left presents in the form of clothes for us since we had behaved well during the year. We were told that Santa Claus had keys to every house in the village and therefore would unlock the doors and leave presents for children who obeyed their parents. In the morning we were too eager to trace the tracks of Santa Claus but in vain. As a child, I belonged to the world of the insatiably curious. Thus, curiosity always got the better of me. I asked my parents to show me the footsteps of Santa Claus. They told me that Santa was like an angel, he flew. Of course, that subterfuge is unlikely to work today, what with our techno-exuberant kids who at the slightest excuse press the mouse button to verify such information on the internet. Nevertheless, during our time the trick worked as we were very motivated to be well-behaved in anticipation of presents at Christmas. This is a typical example of carrots working better than sticks.

In the village Christmas was time for festivities. The village was borderless. Residents would move from home to home as they enjoyed food. No one would be denied food. Strangers would also be welcome. Even penny pinchers would loosen their pockets during Christmas. Those with razor sharp appetites would feed like it was going out of fashion. Tea was prepared in a huge metal bucket in anticipation of many visitors. I remember my mother was at pains in explaining that she prepared lots of food because she anticipated many visitors on Christmas day. Most households would each buy a dozen loaves of bread and a crate of assorted drinks. Chicken was a delicacy eaten mostly at Christmas. Feasting on rice and free-range chicken or what this writer prefers to call chickens without borders, was the apogee of the festivities' culinary pursuits. It could never be Christmas without rice and chicken.

We would all go to church on Christmas day. Almost all congregants at the Vungwi Methodist Church would wear new clothes. It had become more of a fashion extravaganza. My parents, uncles, and aunties who impressed with their dress sense usually formed a choir at Christmas. The choir would sing in church to a thunderous ovation. My uncle who lived in Bulawayo (Zimbabwe's second largest city) was the choir master. He really enjoyed that role. Our parents were showered with Christmas presents by their friends. I remember carrying home a basket full of presents after the church service. They (our parents) would also give presents to their friends during Christmas. These were relations of reciprocity. They were premised on the Shona proverb, *kandiro kanopfumba kunobva kamwe* (one good turn deserves another).

During most of the Christmas services, the preacher was an uncle of ours who went by the title *MuVhangeri* (Evangelist). The *VaVhangeri* (Evangelists) were celebrities in the village. They were sacred cows. Even if they aired, people chose to see no evil, speak no evil, and hear no evil about the *VaVhangeri's* misdemeanours. To most of the congregants, the *VaVhangeri* were immune to sin. It was no surprise that prospective daughters and sons-in-law fell over each other in a bid to catch the eyes of the *VaVhangeri's* sons and daughters. Most of the *VaVhangeri* had acquired a high level of education. A high level of education during those days meant Standard Six, which today is equivalent to about two years in high school. They had acquired their education at mission schools.

During their sermons, the *VaVhangeri* would never shy from showing off their proficiency in the English Language. My siblings and I very much looked forward to these sermons. We particularly enjoyed team sermons by the *VaVhangeri* with the help of members of the Men Christian Union (MCU). During one of these team sermons, at a neighbouring church, Timberyard, where our father had become the resident preacher, we were left in stitches. One of the preachers, who we later gathered was named *Va*Chorara, had fallen asleep during the service. When his turn to preach came, he was awoken by a fellow team preacher. He started saying, "*Umfakazi, umfakazi, umfakazi, umfakazi?*" and promptly sat down. He could have repeated the word more than twenty times. We did not know what that meant. The whole church burst into laughter. We later collected that he was of no fixed aboard. He had no family of his own. His family were fellow congregants. *Va*Chorara lived with members of his church. He would move from home to home. During the old days, congregants were very particular about the need to be each other's keeper. Even when he passed, his fellow congregants footed the bill of the expenses of his funeral. *Va*Chorara was not the only homeless member of the church. There were several others who were also looked after by fellow congregants.

Acts of kindness were not only confined to the church but to the village as well. In our village was an elderly woman, who was related to us, named *Mbuya Ma*Siziba (Granny *Ma*Siziba). *Mbuya Ma*Siziba would bring us goodies in a bag. Her bag was a treasure trove of delights. But its best days were long gone. The bag had patches of brown, blue, green, and white. I remember during later years when I had attained my Ordinary Level (Form Four), I jokingly gave it the name "variegated bag" taking a cue from the term variegated leaf, which I had learned from my Biology teacher. But what we appreciated most was that, patches or no patches, the word love was written all over the bag. *Mbuya Ma*Siziba was very loving. The presents she gave us were all in the name of love. She gave love a good name. *Mbuya Ma*Siziba would sing us the song, *Kudenga hakuna roya* (Heaven has no lawyer). I now have hazy recollections about the lyrics, the song probably went something like this:

> *Kudenga hakuna roya*
> Heaven has no lawyer
> *Kudenga wonomira wega*
> You stand on your own in heaven
> *Wogwa kugwa kwakanaka uripano pasi*
> You have to fight the good fight here on earth

My siblings – Caro, Simba, Andrew (now deceased), and Tsitsi - loved the song not because it was good but because it was a harbinger of good things to come. The youngest in our family, Farai was not yet born. We did not mind how long she took singing the song. What mattered for us was to sharpen our appetites in anticipation of the goodies. After the song, *Mbuya Ma*Siziba would then give us guavas or mangoes, depending with which fruit was in season. Also contained in the bag were roasted peanuts. We got most of these presents from her during Christmas time.

Christmas was also time to welcome the cosmopolitan travellers – the storks. We would marvel at the storks as they went about their usual business of eating grasshoppers in the vlei. With the resident egrets also in attendance, the vlei was painted black and white. It was such a beautiful wildlife spectacle. Occasionally, we would disturb their peace as we chased them. Legend in the village had it that a certain man became very wealthy after spotting and catching a stork with a ring in its leg. One year, when the storks migrated to Europe a very rich man is said to have caught a stork and inserted a ring in one of its legs. According to the legend, if the stork was to be caught when it migrated to Africa, the person who caught it would be given a huge sum of money. The stork was said to have been caught somewhere in east Africa and the person who caught it is said to have earned instant riches. Thus, the legend did not escape our attention. Eagle-eyed as we thought we were, we would spend a few hours looking for the talismanic stork with the ring. Our efforts did not yield positive outcomes. But we had great determination. Only the grumbling of our tummies would make us give up the search. After reloading our tummies, we would be back in the vlei. Eventually, we realised that ours was a wild goose chase and with the advent of winter, the storks were on their travels again. We soon forgot about the search for the ring.

It so happened that our cousin, Miriam had visited her maternal grandmother in Chiwundura about 70 km to the north of our village. We terribly missed her. Holidays without Miriam were boring. When the holidays were about two weeks old, Miriam came back in a blaze of glory. On the following day, very early in the morning, Miriam visited us. She was bubbly and had many stories to tell us. One story which caught our imagination was about storks. Miriam told us that if one would say, *"Gidha mangauzane"* (run storks), the storks would run like sprinters competing in a 100m race at the Olympics. Cousin Miriam was indefatigable when it came to this story. She would demonstrate how the storks ran for hours on end. We instantly believed Miriam's story. There was no room to disbelieve her, for she was a great charmer.

During the rainy season, there was an ephemeral stream in the vlei. The rainy season marked the breeding season of fish. The fish would flow upstream and the local boys had a field day catching the fish but only after one of our brothers Stondido had caught enough fish to fill his bucket. Stondido had a voracious appetite for fish. We heard that one day his wife burned the fish after she forgot to remove the pot of fish from the fire. Apparently, she had gone to the well to fetch some water. When Stondido came back home from the local business centre and found the fish burned, all hell broke loose. The wife had to run for dear life with Stondido hotly in pursuit.

Entertainment was never in short supply in the village. Occasionally, fights would break out in the village, especially after revellers had had more than their fair share of the locally home brewed beer known as "seven days". The beer took seven days to brew hence the name "seven days". There were experts in the village who brewed the beer to the satisfaction of village connoisseurs. The drinking beer at the village pubs known as *ndari*, occasionally ended with fist fights. However, the fights did not end with bloodied noses. After a few skirmishes, "honest brokers" would step in and restore calm. The two most feared fighters were Dhuvayi and Kunga. Pound for pound, these two were evenly matched. Most of the revellers kept their distance from these two. At times however, in the evenings, revellers would break into song. We enjoyed these songs. One of the songs we enjoyed most was, *Doro renyu rinonaka* (The beer is well brewed). Both men and women partook of *ndari*. But mostly it was *chembere* (the elderly) who frequented *ndari*. For *chembere*, it was time to be merry. My paternal grandfather earned himself the nickname, Mukombegumi (ten mugs of beer) for his drinking prowess. He was a regular feature at *ndari*. But *ndari* was not for free. It was a way of raising funds to pay fees for school children. Parents managed to educate their children with proceeds from *ndari*. Young boys who were enterprising would raise money at *ndari* by selling mice kebabs to revellers. As alcohol began to take its toll on the revellers, they would form impromptu choirs and compete with each other. The winners would be given free beer. But it was not a winner takes all scenario. The beer would be shared, true to the egalitarian nature of village life.

Choral music was very popular back in the day. Would-be lovers met during choral music competitions. Choral music was indeed the food of love as Shakespeare would say. School choirs were engaged in a battle royal during choral music competitions. I remember attending one such competition when I was young. My father took me to the competition by virtue of him being the chairman of the local chapter of the Rhodesian African Teachers Association (RATA). It was my first time to attend a competition of that magnitude. The set piece was, *Feluna*. It was a song about a young man who had found his love, presumably of a lifetime. My former classmates and I still sing the song on the few occasions we meet. The song goes something like this:

> *Moyo wangu uzere nemufaro*
> My happiness realises no bounds
> *Nokuti ndawana wandaitsvaka*
> Because I have found the woman of my dreams
> *Feluna, mudiwa wangu wandinodisa*
> Feluna, the woman I love so much
> *Chitima chachazotitora*
> We will board a train
> *Toenda nacho kure-kure*
> Which will take us far
> *Kwandichazondotukwa ndakazvinyararira*

Where Feluna will be taught about values of her new family.

Music played a pivotal role in rituals of courtship. When boys and girls met to play, matters of the heart took centre stage. Declaring love to girls was not for the faint hearted. Many boys developed cold feet when an opportunity to propose to girls presented itself. However, many boys found an easy way out through the folk song *Sarura wako*, (Choose the one you love). The song was about courtship:

> *Sarura wako kadeya-deya wendoro chena*
> Choose the one you love who has no blemish
> *Sarura wako kadeya-deya wendoro chena*
> Choose the one you love who has no blemish
> *Sarura wako kadeya-deya wendoro chena*

Choose the one you love who has no blemish
Wangu ndiSekai kadeya-deya wendoro chena
My love is Sekai who has no blemish
Wangu ndiSekai kadeya-deya wendoro chena
My love is Sekai who has no blemish
Wangu ndiSekai kadeya-deya wendoro chena
My love is Sekai who has no blemish
Sarura wako kadeya-deya wendoro chena
Choose the one you love who has no blemish
Sarura wako kadeya-deya wendoro chena
Choose the one you love who has no blemish
Sarura wako kadeya-deya wendoro chena
Choose the one you love who has no blemish
Wangu ndiKiri kadeya-deya wendoro chena
My love is Kiri who has no blemish
Wangu ndiKiri kadeya-deya wendoro chena
My love is Kiri who has no blemish
Wangu ndiKiri kadeya-deya wendoro chena
My love is Kiri who has no blemish

In as much as the song was sung when boys and girls were playing, the message got home. If, say, a boy chose Sekai, he would try to see how she responded and this made life easier for the suitor if the response was encouraging. Groundwork would have been done for the eventual onslaught. The proposal would then be a mere formality. Other boys, however, chose to write letters proposing love from girls. The address would not be the postal one, the boys would write, "Greenland of love". Others would add, "Kiss before you open" on the envelope. Other suitors would make rather weird requests. They would instruct recipients to revolve 10 times before opening the letters. It was not clear whether the recipients would comply with the requests. I suspect recipients under the influence of Cupid would.

Choral music also played a pivotal role in motivating people to work. This was evidenced during *humwe* (work parties). Tilling the land was mainly done communally during *humwe*. On the day of the *humwe*, villagers who were well-endowed with golden voices led fellow villagers in song. The *humwe* was a show of solidarity. Neighbours were each other's keeper. In the course of the farming season, an individual would invite his/her neighbours to help in cultivating his/her crops. During the *humwe*, village jesters – entertainers extraordinaire - kept other villagers motivated. Laughs came thick and fast. Resultantly, people would not tire, they would work like Trojan horses to finish the day's work.

At times, village life had its fair share of problems mainly associated with witchcraft. Accusations and counter-accusations among relatives was the order of the day. If a person passed on in the village, relatives of the deceased would visit a traditional healer who would do a "post-mortem". A "post-mortem" meant the traditional healer would use his magical "powers" to establish the causes of the deceased's death. In most cases a relative or relatives would be accused for having caused the demise of the deceased. Practice in witchcraft was a blot in the copybook of village life. Life in the village, however, was mostly exciting.

However, the years of unalloyed bliss in the village came to a screeching halt with the advent of war, Zimbabwe's liberation struggle of the 1970s. The 1970s witnessed an influx of the country side by liberation fighters. There were many pitched battles with *vakomana* and *vasikana* (liberation fighters as they were known in the villages) on one hand against the Rhodesian soldiers. The war was brutal, and villagers suffered heavy casualties. This led to the depopulating of the villages. Some villagers escaped to the safety of the towns where they sought refuge. The war finally ended with the British brokered Lancaster House Agreement in 1979 paving way for independence the following year. With the advent of independence, urbanisation began to take its toll on the rural population. Some families relocated to the urban areas to seek opportunities, thus life has since undergone transformation. Closely knitted African families are now few. Gone are the days of families living communally. Individualism has taken root on the rural landscape. These are the realities that crossed my mind as I listened to the roaring ocean at one of the popular beaches in Port Alfred.

As I drove back to Grahamstown, I realised that the golden era of my days as a child growing up in rural pre-independent Zimbabwe are gone. Society is always in constant flux. The bliss associated with village life appears to have gone the way of the dinosaur. Life is not a crystal stair. Life is never perfect. Life twists and turns. Life zigs and zags.

2
The day "Geography" got us into trouble

Geography was the name of my Uncle Aaron's prized bull. Majestic and powerfully built, Geography was the undisputed "heavyweight champion" in the village and beyond. This was the heyday of bull fights. My uncle gave his bull an English name. He was a renowned educationist and took pride in his English accent. They did not nickname him "British" for nothing. English words rolled off his tongue effortlessly. We have to hark back to the days when speaking English in the village was a sign of having scaled the academic ladder. At the slightest excuse, both the educated and the uneducated would use English during various events in the village without regard to the level of English proficiency of their audience. Mostly, the audience comprised the elderly who would acknowledge the unrelenting bombardment orchestrated by their kith and kin, by nodding their heads despite the fact that they could not make head and tail of what their "esteemed" relatives were saying. Never mind that in some cases the English was broken.

My uncle together with those of his ilk, the educated elite belonged to the emerging class of the black middle class. They drove what appeared to the generality in the village, to be sleek cars. They had the luxury of employing domestic workers. Their food was cooked by maids because in most cases the wives were gainfully employed either as nurses or teachers. Some wives were not employed though, thus employing domestic workers was a status symbol. Their lawns were neatly manicured. Maintaining a lawn was a symbol of prestige.

The black middle class were well-educated. Some of them had gone to South Africa to attain education. Some went to the University of Fort Hare in Alice. Some went to Adams College. Others went to Roma University in Lesotho. They came back home armed to teeth with their degrees. They never shied from showing off their academic regalia. A few others, the rare breed, the finest of the fine, managed to enrol at the then University of Rhodesia and Nyasaland. This inspired the younger generation to follow in their footsteps.

The middle class were conspicuous with their western dress. Always clad in suits, they were the talk of the village. When they drove to the villages, they would get a lot of presents from their relatives. The presents included food grown by the villagers. But some of the educated elite had come to assume exotic tastes, thanks to their education. They no longer ate food eaten in the village. They carried their cutlery when they visited the village. When served with food in the village they would use their cutlery (fork and knife) to eat *sadza* (thick maize meal porridge) much to the amusement of their uneducated hosts. Word would spread like fire on a dry prairie about the eating habits of the educated elite.

Most of the educated elite owned livestock. They kept good quality breeds of bulls to improve the quality of cattle. The educated gave their cows, names especially English ones. These bulls had names. Cattle are given names in the village, thereby illustrating the close relationship between villagers and their livestock. Cattle names are symbolic of an event. At times cattle names are symbolic of rivalries between families, while other names are symbolic of the colour or physical features of the cow. For instance, my father's first cow was named *Runyanga* because it had one horn, the other had been broken, presumably as punishment because it had strayed into someone's garden and helped itself with the vegetables. At some stage my father named his other cow Leave because he had used proceeds from his paid leave to buy it. However, I am not sure why my uncle named his bull Geography. My suspicion was that Geography could have been one of his favourite subjects. Whatever the situation was, there was history to cattle names. Each cow's name conveyed a story. The villagers' lives are storied.

In the villages, the most prized bull would be referred to by the clan's totem, e.g. *Dube* for the Zebra totem. In some cases, a spirit medium was said to reside in the bull thereby encapsulating the Shona's concept of the living dead. When the bull had sired a lot of offspring and was old, it would be slaughtered. But the ancestors had to "agree" to the bull's fate. The elder in the clan would pour water on the bull. If it shook its body, the ancestors had "agreed" that it be slaughtered. The village's most prized bull would therefore not make an inglorious exit. Ancestors had to give their consent.

Geography, though not inhabited by an ancestral spirit, commanded respect because of its sheer size and fighting prowess. Geography was our hero. It had a faithful following in the village. I was an ardent member of the "Geography Fan Club". Each time I heard that Geography was involved in a fight, I would take to my heels so as to witness first hand, Geography demolishing an opponent. It had become routine for Geography to vanquish all and sundry. We had become so confident about Geography's assured victories.

One day, a neighbouring village of the Shoko people decided that enough was enough of their bull being humiliated by Geography. They kept a bull that went by the moniker, Foreman, presumably named after George Foreman, a heavyweight champion of the 1970s from the United States of America. Foreman the bull, had, had a chequered history as a fighter. It had its fair share of wins and losses. When the Shoko brought it to our village for the fight with Geography, there could only be one outcome – a Geography win.

The Shoko were of the monkey totem. They were not amused that their bull, Foreman had lived in the shadow of Geography for so long. They never saw themselves as inferior to our village. They were a proud lot. The Shoko people had a score to settle with our village. Our village had more educated people than theirs. We had more accomplished farmers, the *hurudza*, than them. The Shoko people were spoiling for a fight. The two protagonists were supposed to settle the old scores. The two bulls stared at each other for a while as if seizing each other up. Immediately the fight ensured. The mother of all battles had started. They locked horns, puffed, and bellowed thunderously. The bulls appeared to be evenly matched. We cheered on Geography. There was whistling from both sides. At the half-hour mark, Foreman unleashed a blow that sent Geography sprawling into a nearby river. Sodden and distraught, Geography walked out of the river, staggering like a punch-drunk pugilist and promptly slept under the shade of a *Muchakata* tree. The impossible had happened. Water was following upstream. Geography had lost the fight. Yes, Geography had lost to Foreman. But the loss came at a huge cost to Geography. One of its horns had been broken and Geography was bleeding profusely. The boys from my village could not believe this. We felt inadequate. We felt humiliated. There was jubilation from the camp of the victors. For us, Geography was never supposed to be a loser. Geography was a winner. We looked forward to the day Geography would recover and rule the roost. We were not brought up to be despair addicts. We were supposed to remain sanguine and hope for the best.

However, unknown to us, Rhodesian soldiers were watching us. One of my cousins alerted us about the men in military fatigues observing us from a distance using pairs of binoculars. The soldiers were part of a convoy of about five military trucks heading into the countryside. They suspected that we were *mujibhas* (sentinels). *Mujibhas* were the sentinels for the freedom fighters. They conveyed messages to freedom fighters about the presence of the Rhodesian soldiers in an area, the type of weaponry the soldiers were carrying, the number of the soldiers etc. Sensing danger, two of my cousins and I decided to run away from the scene of the bull fight. The speed with which we took off could have made Usain Bolt green with envy. We did not talk to each other as we ran, all we wanted was to get home.

When we were about 500m away from home, a truck zoomed past us and immediately stopped. We continued running. We were shell-shocked to see that the passengers of the civilian car were Rhodesian soldiers. They were ten in all, seven were white, and three were black. "*Hupi logandanga?*" (Where are the freedom fighters?), yelled a white soldier in broken Shona. "*Ngayiuye pano*" (Come here), thundered another white soldier. Before we knew it, we were bundled into the truck and taken to the main road where the rest of the soldiers were. We were asked to sit on the rails of the army trucks and the torture started. They burned us with cigarettes. They beat the daylights out of us. We started crying hoping that they would stop beating us. But the beating intensified. We were accused of being *mujibhas* despite the fact that we were too young to be involved in such an onerous task. The soldiers' thinking was that when we ran away from the scene of the bullfight, we were running to tell the freedom fighters about the presence of soldiers in our locality. For them, stopping us in our tracks was a pre-emptive strike meant to prevent freedom fighters from ambushing them.

After about three hours, we were released. We tried to run but our feet had become swollen because of the beating. We walked away but with difficult. Tears were flowing down our cheeks. What wrong had we done to our assailants, we wondered. How could five truckloads of heavily armed soldiers pounce on very small defenceless and innocent boys? We could not fathom that injustice meted on us.

Meanwhile the village rumour mill had not been idle. The rumour mill was mainly powered by *Tete* (aunt) Dhora. She was an incurable gossip. The moment she opened her mouth, she churned out venom. Aunt Dhora was indefatigable when it came to rumour mongering. Thus, when we had been taken by the soldiers, aunt Dhora had told the villagers about our story. How aunt Dhora got wind of the story is a mystery. Suffice to say she always had her ears to the ground. According to her, we had been forcibly taken by soldiers to *kumakomba*. *Kumakomba* were pits dug for the purposes of interrogating and torturing suspected freedom fighters and war collaborators during Zimbabwe's liberation struggle. Others said we had been taken to an army barracks in Gweru and some villagers claimed that we had been beaten and left unconscious.

After we had been released by the soldiers, we decided to go at a nearby home which belonged to our uncle. We found my uncle and his family crying. They could not believe that we were still alive. Our auntie immediately boiled water with herbs to administer on our swollen feet. We were also given food since we had not eaten anything since morning. Our uncle asked us to give our side of the story about what had taken place. We gave a narration about the bullfight between Geography and Foreman. One of our uncle's children, Majaya

Mhuri, hardly out of nappies, appeared to be "listening" attentively. The word that caught his attention was Geography but because he was young, he mispronounced the word as *Joglaf.* My cousins and I nicknamed him *Joglaf.* He is now a grown-up man. The nickname has stuck on him like a bad breath.

Our parents heard that we were at our uncle's place and they all came to see us. My cousins and I started crying. My parents took me home and assured me that I would be fine. They told me that I should count myself lucky to be alive. Many innocent people had perished because of the war. I could not hide my joy for being free at last. The ordeal at the hands of the Rhodesian soldiers stretched my resolve to pray for Geography's recovery so as to challenge Foreman.

3
The village 800-pound gorilla

Munhuwepi was the village head of Musasa. He loved power. He could do anything to have power. Over the years, he had become desensitised to lies. Thus, most of the villagers took everything Munhuwepi said with a pinch of salt. Also known for his hair trigger temper, he had become a polarising figure in the village. Some villagers had since accepted him as he was, while others were alienated by his antics. His time as village head amounted to a reign of terror. Maximillian Robespierre would have smiled in his grave. But his fiercely loyal hangers-on portrayed him as a victim of a rival clan vying for the headship of the village.

Born to a happy-go-lucky and polygynous father, Munhuwepi detested beer drinking. He attributed his father's irresponsible behaviour to alcohol consumption. Growing-up in the village, Munhuwepi dreamt of a future with a wife and children, since to him, a polygynous marriage was anathema. But true to the adage that an apple does not fall far from the tree, Munhuwepi married two wives, *Ma*Ndlovhu and Hwiza. *Ma*Ndlovhu was hardworking and spent most of the time tilling her fields. She produced a lot of grain. Most of the grain was consumed by her family and surplus grain was sold.

Hwiza on the other hand was lazy and spent most of her time beer drinking. She made the begging bowl her companion. Each time other villagers saw her coming to their homes, they knew Hwiza would ask for grain. Those full of the milk of human kindness would donate food to her. Others, whose patience had been stretched to the limit, no longer cared about her. But they could not do anything to her for fear of victimisation. Year in and year out, Hwiza remained the village beggar. She was ridiculed by other villagers, though in hushed tones.

Also known as *Mapedzahama*, because she was accused of practising witchcraft, Hwiza was a very unpopular figure in the village. It was said that she gave a look that would instantly freeze boiling water. Hwiza was accused of bewitching several people in the village. She did not take kindly to these allegations. She would unleash an expletive-laden tirade against her accusers. Many villagers had learned to avoid getting involved in a bare-knuckled fight with her. It was prudent to do so. One would not want to earn the wrath of the village head. The village head would humiliate his wife's adversaries at village gatherings. At times village meetings turned into kangaroo courts meant to discipline people who had fallen out of favour with the village head.

Why Munhuwepi married her is difficult to comprehend. Some villagers thought that Hwiza used *mupfuhwira* (love enhancing charm) to have a stranglehold on her husband. Others speculated that Hwiza knew Munhuwepi's secrets that included a rumour that he had murdered a vagabond. Therefore, Munhuwepi could not antagonise Hwiza because he feared that she could spill the beans. Thus, Hwiza remained a sacred cow in the village. Despite the bravado Munhuwepi tried to show in the village, he was a mere grasshopper when it came to his relationship with Hwiza. This was not lost to Hwiza who would always boast about it. Besides, Munhuwepi had sired 13 children, all boys, with Hwiza. One would be forgiven for thinking that the rate at which they were prolific with babies would put rabbits to shame. But as per dictates of patriarchal societies, a wife's worthiness to a clan was judged by the number of sons she bore.

In the village, Munhuwepi rode roughshod over the villagers. His reign as village head was characterised by delusional grandeur. He treated other villagers like they were chattel. They were forced to attend marathon meetings, ostensibly for discussing issues to do with development in the village. During these meetings, Munhuwepi dominated all proceedings and did not tolerate dissenting voices, it was his way or the highway. He threatened to expel any disloyal subjects. His ideas would always prevail.

Forming buttresses around him were his so-called advisers – Moyondizvo, Tichagwa, and Chengaose. The three men would simply rubberstamp his decisions. All they wanted was to please their superior. Of the three, the most prominent bootlicker was Moyondizvo. He volunteered to look after the village head's livestock each time the herd boy was not available. However, it seems it was an Orwellian definition of volunteer. Each time the herd boy was not available, the village head would visit Moyondizvo and tell him about his (Munhuwepi) predicament. Moyondizvo would have no option but "volunteer" to look after the cattle. After the agricultural season, Moyondizvo showered the village head with presents of bags of maize and groundnuts. Moyondizvo did everything he could to make the village head happy. He knew his loyalty would translate into benefits and protection especially during times of scarcity.

In the same village was a well-respected septuagenarian named Towonga. Towonga was a man ennobled by generosity. He helped with school fees, many people in the village who could not afford to send their children to school. Towonga had had an illustrious career as an educationist for over 40 years. Of the 40, 30 years were spent as a headmaster. He was said to have been very talented as an English speaker. His proficiency as an English speaker earned many posts during his teaching career. At one stage he served as the chairman of the local chapter of the teachers' organisation named the Rhodesian African Teachers' Association for 20 years until his retirement. Many villagers looked up to him for advice. This did not go down well with Munhuwepi the village head. He became very jealousy to an extent that he did not hide it.

In response, Towonga would tell other villagers that nobody could take a God given talent. He would make reference to a popular song, entitled, *Mupata waChidembo* (The Civet cat's Pass) by popular singer Kiren Zulu. In the song, Kiren Zulu sings about how a civet cat died on a mountain pass. Subsequently, the pass was named *Mupata waChidembo* (The Civet Cat's Pass). This did not go down well with *Nhoro* (Kudu). *Nhoro* was very jealousy that a mountain pass in the locality had been named after Chidembo (civet cat). One day Nhoro fell ill on the pass named after Chidembo, and died. Nhoro thought that if he died on the same pass, it would be renamed *Mupata waNhoro* (Kudu's Pass). Instead people went in droves to the pass to collect meat of the kudu. People would say, "Let's go to *Mupata waChidembo*" (The Civet Cat's Pass) to collect meat of a dead kudu. Nobody renamed the pass after the kudu. The message in the song is that nobody can take a talent from someone. Towonga's message was a thinly veiled attack on Munhuwepi. His message was that Munhuwepi could not take away his God given talent. In response, Munhuwepi worked round the clock to make alliances with anyone who could help him "discipline" his rivals.

Munhuwepi cultivated very close relations with the liberation fighters. He was the fighters' confidante. He knew their whereabouts, where they cached arms and gave them vital information about the movements of the Rhodesian soldiers thereby earning their (liberation fighters)' trust. Munhuwepi took advantage of his close relationship with the fighters to settle scores with his enemies. He accused his enemies of being sell-outs and that they would be disciplined by the liberation fighters. The crucial support he got from the liberation fighters helped Munhuwepi to crush dissent. Munhuwepi claimed he got military training from the liberation fighters. To the villagers, he had become one of the fighters. He would order villagers to prepare dishes of *sadza* (thick maize meal porridge) served with free range chicken. He claimed the meals were meant for the liberation fighters. Suddenly, he no longer ate *sadza* served with vegetables. The villagers obeyed his orders. What else could they do? Munhuwepi had the whole village eating out of his hand.

During the liberation war, villagers no longer had freedom to make merry at *ndari*. Village life had become unbearable and some villagers migrated to the urban areas. This was vividly captured by the legendary Zimbabwean musician Thomas Mapfumo's song *Chiruuzevha Chapera*. The lyrics of this song are as follows:

> *Hereri baba*
> Dear father
> *Chirizevha chapera*
> Rural life has ended
> *Chirizevha chapera*
> Rural life has ended
> *Chirizevha chapera*
> Rural life has ended
> *Hinga zvinonzwisa tsitsi mambo*
> It's a sad situation dear Lord
> *Vamwe vakatiza hondo kumusha uko*

Some ran away from the war in the rural areas
Vamwe vakadimbuka makumbo
Some were paralysed because of the war

In the post-independence era, the title, krall head was discontinued because of its colonial connotations. The term village head replaced the title of krall head. Munhuwepi thought he had been elevated by this new title. But nothing had really changed as explained by an old African saying that a bird that flies from the ground and lands on an anthill does not know that it is still on the ground.

Munhuwepi continued to exercise his stranglehold on the villagers. During drought years he would use drought relief to consolidate his power. Villagers who did not support his line of thinking were denied food handouts. In this respect, Munhuwepi worked in cohorts with Togara and *Ma*Mpofu the village secretary. These three constituted the village's axis of evil. Villagers who crossed Munhuwepi's path were not given grain. This has been characteristic of Munhuwepi's village headship over the years.

His hangers-on, would not miss out on food handouts. Munhuwepi had a girlfriend, Magariro in the neighbouring village of Mavhundira. Some of the grain meant for people in his village was given to Magariro. Magariro became a subject of ridicule in both villages of Mavhundira and Musasa. She wore a thick skin and did not care about what people said as long as she continued to get a supply of food from Munhuwepi. Magariro was known for her fighting skills. Her bite was more effective than her bark. At last, Hwiza had met her match. Hwiza would grumble within a safe distance. She could not dare come out in the open because she could be added as a statistic to the list of Magariro's casualties.

Such were characteristics of Munhuwepi's long "reign" as village head. But Munhuwepi, the village 800-pound gorilla could not defy time. His biological clock continues to tick relentlessly. Munhuwepi now ravaged by geriatric ailments, looks crestfallen. He spends most of his time "cultivating" his garden, reminiscing about a by-gone era. At times he talks to himself, apparently indicative of a person who has gone off the rails.

4
The bee's knees from Shurugwi

Zimbabwe's capital Harare, is a cultural bouillabaisse. In the 1980s, touted as the sunshine city, people from all over the world trekked to Harare to enjoy their place in the sun. Three decades into independence, the sun appeared to be no longer shining on the capital. Economic malaise had taken root. However, with crisis comes opportunities. The Ruvheneko sisters – Topiwa, Totenda and Todiwa joined the "Great Trek" to the capital where through a combination of luck, shady deals and sheer determination, they met with success. Elegant and well-heeled, they have climbed the social ladder and made names for themselves in Harare's melting pot.

They did part of their primary education at Railway Block School in Shurugwi where their parents were teachers. With the uncertainty surrounding the future of the chrome mines in Shurugwi because of sanctions imposed on the Rhodesian government, Mr and Mrs Ruvheneko left Railway Block School. They moved to rural Shurugwi to take up teaching posts at Vungwi School. Mr and Mrs Ruvheneko moved with their three daughters. However, it took a while for their daughters to adjust to rural life. There was no tape water in the rural areas. There was also no electricity.

The sisters could not carry buckets of water on their heads. They found it funny that girls of their age in the village could carry water buckets on their heads. On the other hand, most of the girls in the village could not comprehend how the Ruvheneko sisters could not do simple chores such as carrying water on one's head. The Ruvheneko sisters soon became the laughing stock in the village. The girls were not disturbed of being caricatured. The sisters still regarded themselves as urbanites and did not care a hoot what the other girls in the village thought about them. Totenda, Todiwa, and Topiwa were amply endowed with good looks. They more than compensated their lack of skills with their haunting beauty. At school, lily-livered boys could only dream of going out with the three beauties. One needed to be very courageous to approach them.

Fashion-wise, the three sisters were pacesetters. They were fashion addicts. Their parents would take them to Gweru to buy clothes at the end of each month. In Gweru, they would visit their favourite restaurant – Midlands Fish and Chips. Of the three, Topiwa was the pickiest. She did not settle for any type of food. Topiwa loved to eat fish and chips. Topiwa claimed that not eating fish was bad for her health. There are times when she feigned illness, ostensibly to force her parents to take her to Gweru and buy her favourite food, fish and chips. The other two did not mind the food their parents bought them. They were more concerned about the quality of clothes they wore.

Todiwa was the most gifted academically. In 1976, the Shurugwi district launched a yearly competition for the number ones of each class for every school. For example, the number ones in grade five for every school in the district would meet and write a test. The student with the best results would then be declared the number one of all the grade fives. Todiwa came out first at Vungwi in the grade five class and represented the school at the district level. And true to form, Todiwa came out tops of all the grade five students in the district that same year. She had created an aura of invincibility. Todiwa had announced her arrival in style. She had become one of the most talked about students at the school and for the right reasons.

This accomplishment was a poster child for what was in the offing. Her parents pinned a lot of hope on her and saw her scaling academic heights. The other two, Topiwa and Totenda we also gifted in class. They were in the top five in their respective classes. Although not as gifted as their sibling, nonetheless, they were a force to reckon with at the school. Thus, the Ruvheneko sisters were well respected at the school. In the village, they were envied by every parent. Who would not have loved to have children as good in class as the three sisters? Some parents had become even jealousy of the achievements of the sisters. With knives sharpened, they plotted against the Ruvheneko girls like a pack of Judases Iscariot.

As if to confirm this conspiracy, Totenda fell ill. The parents took her to doctors in Gweru, but her condition did not improve. One of the uncles, Mapfupa, a traditional healer would bring herbs to heal Totenda. Each time the uncle would come, Totenda would cry saying that she was seeing a witch riding a hyena. The parents were so unhappy with the presence of the uncle. The uncle was well-known in the village, allegedly for witchcraft. His mother was said to have been a much feared witch. People spoke in hushed tones about her having bewitched a very affable elderly woman known as Gwatiringa. Some of the villagers argued that when Mapfupa's mother died, she passed the tools of the (witchcraft) trade to her son. Already, fingers had been pointed at Mapfupa when two villagers died in mysterious circumstances. It did not come as a surprise therefore, that Mr and Mrs Ruvheneko suspected that Mapfupa had bewitched their daughter. Mapfupa heard about the allegation and threatened to report Mr and Mrs Rhuvheneko to the chief. Accusations and counter accusations flew across the *ruzhowa* (a 'fence' made of thorny branches) separating their homesteads.

Mapfupa's children were not good in class. They were perennial tail-enders. Thus, each time Mapfupa heard about the school results of the Ruvheneko girls, he would beat up his children accusing them of being dull. But Mapfupa is said to have left school while he was doing grade three. It was also rumoured that he was never known for academic prowess. No wonder then that apples do not fall far away from the tree. All in all, Mapfupa had seven known children but with different women. His womanising was legendary. Legend had it that he used charms to lure unsuspecting women, regardless of their marital status. Families are said to have broken-up because of his shenanigans. Mapfupa was not well liked in the village, but he had a handful of followers who thronged his homestead for herbs and charms. Some of these followers ganged-up with Mapfupa against the Ruvheneko family. They accused the Ruvhenekos of being a proud family.

With time, Totenda recovered. The parents attributed the recovery to their faith in God. They were regular worshippers at the local Methodist church. They took their daughters to church every Sunday. Totenda and Todiwa sang in the junior choir. They also led the church in the praise and worship session. They only quit the choir after they had started their high school. They went to different schools. Totenda and Todiwa both went to Loreto High School about 80 km from their home. Topiwa did her high school at Dadaya Mission. After high school, she got a job as a bank teller in Harare. Topiwa rose through the ranks to become a branch manager. She applied for a loan and bought a house in Harare's Mount Pleasant suburb. Her other two sisters enrolled at the University of Zimbabwe. Totenda did Psychology and went on to do an MSc in Clinical Psychology in Australia. When she came back home she worked for a non-governmental organisation. After a while, she bought a fleet of eight haulage trucks known locally as *magonyeti*. Through her international networks, Totenda got a lucrative contract for her fleet of haulage trucks to ferry goods in the southern African region. Her pockets soon became bottomless.

Totenda was living large. She was big news in the village. How she got money to buy the haulage trucks was subject to speculation. Back in the village, there were several theories about how Totenda made her fortune. The theory that found currency was that she was involved in diamond dealing with some foreign nationals. *Mangoda* (diamonds) were discovered in the eastern part of the country thereby triggering a diamond rush. Many fortune seekers from all over the world invaded the diamond fields. Some became rich while others only managed meagre pickings from the rush.

Todiwa did a BSc in Environmental Science. After which she was awarded a fellowship to enrol for an MSc Environmental Management at the University of Cape Town in South Africa. After her masters, Todiwa enrolled at Columbia University in the United States for a PhD, which she successfully completed and came back home. After a difficult period of job-hunting, Todiwa at long last got her *emploi de rêve*. She got a job as a lecturer at one of the local universities. She also got numerous consultancy jobs. Dr Todiwa Ruvheneko was talked about in the village but she was not as revered as Totenda. Villagers were in awe of Totenda because she had made a lot of money. Although the educated are respected in the village, the moneyed call the shots, true to the Shona saying, *ane mari ndiye mukuru* (He/she who has money pulls the strings). Thus, because the sisters have money, they have become very influential.

In Harare, the Ruvheneko sisters go to the Rosebank International Pentecostal Church in the city centre. They made a name for themselves because of the help they gave to the church. Affectionately known as the "Big 3 at Rosebank", the sisters would not hesitate to flex their financial muscle when duty called, much to the appreciation of the resident minister.

However, time and again, juicy stuff would be said about the sisters. One very uncomplimentary story about the sisters was how they had ill-treated their paternal grandmother before she died. The sisters are said to have accused her of bewitching them. Also doing the rounds in the church, was that the sisters were on a few occasions found to be in a state of inebriation. But they were untouchables. They had money. The church leaders would see no evil, speak no evil, and hear no evil about the sisters. They had the congregants eating out of their hands. The resident minister eulogised them. This is the tragedy of how society has fetishized wealth. In some instances, those who have money curry favours with some men and women of cloth.

For retail therapy, the Ruvheneko sisters' ultimate shopping destination is Cape Town in South Africa. They patronise high-end boutiques at the cathedrals of consumption to flex their sartorial biceps. They hop from mall to mall and shop till the price drops. Their appreciation of latest fashion trends is second to none. Always elegantly dressed, the sisters never fail to impress in their role as fashion pacesetters. When traveling to South Africa, they use South African Airways. They distaste travelling by road as they see it not befitting their social status.

When they are back in village, they mimic the way South Africans speak. To show surprise they say, "*yhuu*" and when not in agreement or happy about something they say, "*hayibo*". "*Yhuu*" and "*hayibo*" have become part of the village lingua - courtesy of the Ruvheneko sisters. This type of language is what one would hear in the Western Cape of South Africa. Villagers who visit *Mzansi* (South Africa) are regarded highly in the village. Some of the villagers who end up living in South Africa create a myth about their social status. They come back home driving flashy cars and live for the day. Because of this ostentatiousness, they earned themselves the nickname *injiva*. Like F Scott Fitzgerald's *nouveau riche*, the *injiva*'s concerns are steeped in partying and spending big at local rural business centres. While the haughty fashionistas, the Ruvheneko sisters, are not *injiva*, they nevertheless are showy. Their different pursuits have earned them wealth.

Besides her fleet of haulage trucks, Totenda also runs a barbecue joint she named City Zollywood. City Zollywood has taken Harare by storm. Revellers who regard themselves as people of high social standing have become permanent features at City Zollywood. The city's socialites are frequent patrons at the entertainment joint. Located about 30 km from the city centre, City Zollywood offers a serene environment, a break from the hustle and bustle of city life. Revellers who frequent City Zollywood drink imported alcohol beverages such as Amstel, Heineken, and Flying Fish. Some prefer imported whiskies in a bid to prove that their pockets are loaded. Revellers show off the type of car they are driving. When relaxing at City Zollywood, they put their car keys on the table, and never in their pockets. This sends a clear message about who is driving the latest top of the range Mercedes Benz, BMW, or SUV. Smart phone addicts not to be outdone, also display their phones on the tables constantly glancing at their pricy gadgets to check WhatsApp and Facebook messages. They have been enslaved by their gadgets. Attention is divided between their friends and their smartphones. No wonder that celebrated historian Yuval Noah Harari has said that modern humans suffer from Fear of Missing out (FOMO).

Revellers at City Zollywood are usually entertained by Zimbabwe superstar musician, Oliver Mtukudzi. His hit song *Mutavara* sends revellers into a trance. The veteran musician, known for his acoustic guitar wizardry, belts out hit after hit sending the revellers into a frenzy. The patrons normally sing along to show adoration to their hero. City Zollywood has become very popular, and thus, is the only game in town. This is further testimony of the success of the Ruvhenekos in contrast to their relatives in the rural areas.

The Ruvhenekos live next to yet another uncle, Mawaya and his family. He has spent most of his adult life doing menial jobs. At some stage he made a living as a traditional healer. This invited a lot of the ridicule from the Ruvhenekos, who accuse him of practising witchcraft. Uncle Mawaya and his wife Zvogozha's children have not done well in comparison. The eldest, Tendayi works as domestic worker at a nearby school. Her salary is not enough to support herself and her son. The rest are not working. Two boys, now young adults spend most of their time at the local business centre accosting for alcohol from potential "donors". They have become a nuisance and are despised by some revellers at the business centre.

Two of Tendayi's younger sisters are said to have disappeared from home and gone to Masvingo, a nearby city to try and earn a living. People in the village do not know what the two are doing in Masvingo. Once in a while, they come back home with a few groceries for their parents. The lives of

Uncle Mawaya and his family are a sharp contrast to their more esteemed relatives, the Ruvhenekos.

There has been bad blood between the two families. Accusations and counter-accusations between the two families have become the norm. Uncle Mawaya and his family suspect that the Ruvhenekos use *tokoloshis* (goblins) to make lots of money. The Ruvhenekos are also accused of casting an evil spell on Uncle Mawaya and his family. On the other hand, the Ruvhenekos accuse Uncle Mawaya of bewitching their ailing parents. Relations between the two families has reached rock-bottom. These are tell-tale signs of a low intensity "cold war" going on. There are no signs of the "cold war" thawing.

The Ruvheneko sisters remain anchored on the upper rungs of the social ladder. They like it that way, for they consider themselves to be the doyens of their clan. They are perched at the top of the clan. For them, happiness is about climbing the social ladder. The sisters are a proud lot. Their pride appears to only rival that of a peacock. Perhaps, they think they are the bee's knees. After all they have money, be it ill-gotten or not. They represent *homo economicus*. They are part of the story of growing inequalities in society. The gap between the rich and those who live on the margins of survival, poignantly and inexorably, continues to grow.

5
Finis Chachacha?

"*Finis* Chachacha", were the first words Rudo, said when we met on a chilly but sun-kissed morning at Chachacha after more than 20 years. Apparently, his message was that Chachacha was now a fading entertainment hub. We were greeted by a screaming billboard with the inscription, "Happy Chachacha". But what we saw told a different story. Buildings were rundown, fences were broken, and the roads were in a state of disrepair. In hind sight the inscription should have read, "Unhappy Chachacha". Clearly, the once thriving business centre looked very "unhappy". Stoney faced revellers told a story of a how the once mighty Chachacha has fallen. A feeling of ennui engulfed us.

Rudo and I were in the same class during our days in junior school. We reminisced about the good old days when we used to meet at Chachacha and play darts. Chachacha is the name generally used to refer to our local business centre. Some people call it Donga while officially I am told it is known as Chitepo. The name Chachacha, however, has stuck. Legend has it that the name Chachacha originated from Zambia and is said to have been a genre of music. In the 1960s and 70s, many Zimbabweans migrated to Zambia which had just attained independence. The liberation struggle in Zimbabwe was beginning to intensify. Resultantly, many young men and women fled to neighbouring countries to join the struggle. Some Zimbabweans were attracted by the magnet of opportunity and became wealthy business people. This was during the time when Zambia's economy was experiencing a boom with copper fetching high prices on the international market. The well-heeled who had made it big in Zambia would come home back to Zimbabwe to invest. Shurugwi was no exception, a local businessman with proceeds from Zambia decided to invest heavily at the local business centre and built a hotel and named it Chachacha. Chachacha soon became a famous entertainment hub.

Rudo and I decided to quench our thirst at a bottle store named, *Peace and Serenity*. Clearly, what we witnessed in the bottle store 30 minutes later, told a different story. Two revellers started a heated argument about which team played better, Arsenal or Tottenham Hotspurs. The Arsenal supporter could not accept that North London's bragging rights were now at White Hart Lane, formerly Tottenham's home ground. A fight immediately started. The fight was soon joined by more revellers according to where their support was between the two teams. Fists flew in the air and there was pandemonium in the bottle store. The fight was eventually stopped by police officers who happened to be passing by.

With "peace and serenity" eventually restored, I engaged a reveller in a discussion. I bought him a few beers and after getting tipsy, he began telling me stories, some of the stories made me conclude that he was a stranger to the truth. For as long as he was assured of more supplies of beer, stories would continue to roll off his tongue. He told me an apocryphal tale of a businessman who is said to have kept human organs in his freezer to attract customers. The businessman is said to have kept the human organs frozen for over twenty-five years. The freezer was kept locked and the only other person who could open it was his wife. The reveller claimed that the human organs were eventually removed by the police after a tip-off from one of his workers. The reveller further claimed that after the human organs were removed the business empire of the businessman collapsed like a deck of cards. Such tales abound at rural business centres. Some business people believe that human organs are talismanic.

The reveller and I began to reflect on the heydays of Chachacha. The 1970s and 80s were Chachacha's halcyon years. All roads converged at Chachacha. Fun loving men would drive all the way from Salisbury (now Harare), about 340 km away, to Chachacha with bevies of beautiful ladies in tow. They were treated to beautiful music by the resident band. Some would end up booked at Chachacha for two weeks. Others would return to buy homes near the business centre, just to be close to the fun.

Bus drivers would stop at Chachacha to have their meals as passengers disembarked from the buses to buy food; thus, business was brisk at Chachacha. This translated into wealth for the local entrepreneurs. They drove the latest cars. We used to cheer one of the business people, Mr Zvionere. He was a very speedy driver and he drove a Ford Fairline. We were in awe of Mr Zvionere.

Meanwhile, we were joined by four other revellers and soon were engaged in a bruising debate about who among the local businesspersons at Chachacha was the richest. What yardstick measured wealth, we wondered? Some thought the quality of clothes the businessperson wore was an indicator of how rich he was. Another reveller said that the size of the business premises were indicative of wealth. Two others said the type of car driven by the businessman was a measure of his wealth. The debate ended in a stalemate, we could not agree on how best wealth was supposed to be measured. In the village however, being pot-bellied and double chinned were signs of wealth for a businessman. The wife of a businessman was supposed be a *sidhudhla* (obese woman) to show that she was married to a wealthy man. By this time the reveller I befriended first was clearly in a drunken stupor. He was now staggering like a punch-drunk pugilist. Rudo and I said goodbyes to each other and I left the bottle store.

Two weeks later, on another visit at Chachacha, I bumped into a kinsman of mine who happens to run a butchery. He talked about the massive housing project going on in the residential areas of Chachacha. The project seems to tell a different story from the reality on the ground. Some businesses are collapsing due to viability problems. Live musical shows are now few. Most of the owners of the buildings are now renting them out. Ambitious unfinished buildings are now twilight spaces of crime.

About 10km to the north east of Chachacha is another business centre popularly known as Chirashavana (abandon children). Revellers would literally abandon their families in pursuit of happiness. Morally deformed men would splash money like confetti at a wedding and spend it with equally immoral women. Most of the revellers would end up at Chachacha, given its magnetic attraction as the ultimate entertainment hub in Shurugwi district.

During Christmas, Chachacha hosted more than its fair share of visitors. On Christmas day parents allowed their children, both boys and girls to have fun at Chachacha. Crowds would start gathering at about 10am. By 3pm, the crowds would swell to several hundreds. It was also time to show off new outfits. Outfits of all shapes and sizes were on display. Herd boys would be given a day off to have fun at Chachacha. It was also a perfect excuse for naughty children to try alcoholic beverages. Alcohol would get the better of them. Some would end up being carried home in a drunken state. In the mornings they would ready themselves for a tongue-lashing session from their parents.

Christmas time at Chachacha was time for reunions. Long lost friends would meet and relive their past. Those perceived to have done well in life would show off their latest "wheels". Inevitably, social stratification would be the norm. Visiting urbanites who had excelled education wise, gathered together and talked about their achievements. They gathered at the "trendy" bars with their sleek cars parked outside. They listened to country music by the likes of Kenny Rogers and Don Williams that was played at low volume to enable the revellers to engage in conversations.

The not so educated would occasionally stray to these "elite" bars to ask for money. They would earn themselves an ear bashing from their more successful relatives who did not want their peace to be disturbed. They would leave with tails between their legs. The herd boys and those of their ilk would frequent the noisy bars were loud music was played. In these bars was both opaque and clear beer. The patrons were rowdy and in most cases fist fights would ensue.

With the economic challenges experienced by the country in the post-colonial era, rural business centres such as Chachacha have been hit the hardest. However, the new housing projects attest to the Chachacha juggernaut and its staying power. With new mining ventures taking place near Chachacha, the business centre is poised to grow. Like the phoenix, Chachacha looks poised to rise from the ashes. But whether its reputation as an entertainment hub will surpass the Chachacha of the pre-independence era, is anybody's guess. *Finis* Chachacha? Perhaps not.

6
A basket of deplorables

For students doing junior school in the village, the dream to attend a boarding school for their secondary education was not just an item on their bucket lists. It meant much more than that, it was their Holy Grail. Attending boarding school enhanced their status symbol. Boarding school attendees were the who's who in the village. Boarding schools of note during the colonial era were mostly mission schools. Among the mission schools were: Dadaya, Waddilove, St Augustine's, Gokomere, Thekwane, St David's Bonda, Kutama, Sanyati, Loreto, Usher, and Kwenda.

Life at a boarding school was exciting. Boarding schools were a melting pot with students of contrasting characters. Some were devout Christians, and these made the Holy Bible their companion. They referred to each other as brothers and sisters. There was seemingly perfect camaraderie among them. The brothers and sisters looked askance on anyone who did not uphold Christian values. Others took to reading like a duck takes to water. Back in the day it was fashionable to go and read outdoors. Roaming the wilds, you would occasionally come across these book worms and they looked rather intimidating with their heaps of voluminous books.

At Dadaya Mission, were students hewn from different cloths. The naughty ones would occasionally slip out of the dormitories to catch a puff of a cigar in Makepesi valley or drink traditional beer from nearby villages. Makepesi valley was the meeting place for smokers. I am not sure how the name Makepesi valley came about. All students bent on mischief making would meet in Makepesi valley. This group of students resented school rules. They were a basket of deplorables. They mostly comprised a group of senior boys who went by the alias, Ndege Brothers. Ndege was the name of a type of opaque beer brewed in the neighbouring town of Zvishavane. Ndege is a Shona word for aircraft. It was said that if an individual got drunk with Ndege, he would "fly" like an aircraft. Men who drank Ndege would not return home for several days. Women are said to have demonstrated that Ndege be banned. After an unrelenting show of power by the women, Ndege was banned. This did not mean the end of the Ndege Brothers, if anything, the boys became more and more popular and were eulogised at their mission school.

Most noticeable among the Ndege Brothers were Kondo, Kambeva, and Mujakatira. I hear these were nicknames. I never got to know their real names. Kondo was incredibly popular among the students at Dadaya because he always deceived them with his butter wouldn't melt in his mouth "innocence". During elections to choose the chairperson of the entertainment committee, Kondo was elected unanimously, beating his rivals hands down. Kondo and his brothers in crime went to celebrate the victory at Mafala, a nearby rural area where there was readily available traditional beer. Because the Ndege Brothers were always broke, they stole clothes hung on the lines at the boys' dormitories. They would then engage in barter trade with the villagers. They would exchange clothes for beer. On this fateful day, their luck ran out. They were caught by the headmaster red-handed. A villager from Mafala had alerted the headmaster of the presence of students drinking alcohol in the village. The Ndege boys were taken back to school by the headmaster. The brothers were given very hard punishment at "Siberia". Students at the mission school were very creative. They gave the name "Siberia" because they had studied the history of Russia. During the 1930's, the Russian leader Joseph Stalin punished the richer peasants, the kulaks because they resisted his policy on collectivisation. The dissenting peasants were forcibly taken to Siberia to do hard labour. Siberia was also inhospitable because of the severe cold weather. This did not escape the creative mind of the students at Dadaya who came up with their own version of "Siberia". At "Siberia" students who had been punished would dig holes as deep as two metres, and a width of the same measurement. During the farming season, students who had broken school rules would weed the school fields at "Siberia".

Thus, when the Ndege brothers were caught by the headmaster, they knew that hard labour was beckoning at "Siberia". The school head was an iron disciplinarian. He did not brook any mischief on the part of students. He called the Ndege Brothers to his office the following day. The brothers were immediately taken to "Siberia" for their punishment. They were to spend the next seven days digging holes. Other students only saw them during lunch hour at the dining hall. The drinking escapade cost Kondo the chairmanship of the entertainment committee. He was replaced by an astute student named Zebediah. Zebediah was one of the sharpest minds at the school. Students were in awe of him. He was well-cultured and won many prizes at the end of every year during his stay at Dadaya.

But the Ndege brothers were not done yet. Mischief came naturally for them. Each time you would see them, trouble was never far away. They would mobilise students to go on strike at the slightest excuse. One day a rumour spread at the school that the number of meals served with meat were to be reduced because of meat price increases. This did not go down well with the "carnivorous" Ndege brothers. They loved their meat. The notorious Ndege Brothers immediately summoned all students to the school hall and called for a strike. Up went barricades, down went the school flag. The strike had started. The lynch mob – the Ndege brothers, Chitanda, perennial student Chidhoma and disgraced former head girl Sluza were directing operations. Sluza made a name for herself as a gifted netballer, she hogged the limelight for her netball prowess in Form One and two. As she grew older, her attempts at trying to outfox time proved futile. She was no longer as agile as she was before and eventually called it quits. Perceived to be a tough disciplinarian, Sluza was appointed head girl at the mission school. However, her reign as head girl was short-lived after she was caught drinking alcohol in Zvishavane by the headmaster. She did not want to fade into the shadows, thus, she decided to show her true colours. She had an axe to grind with the headmaster. She was itching for a revenge. Therefore, the strike was a god send for Sluza. It was no surprise that she would perch herself at the top of the lynch mob.

The headmaster immediately ordered the closure of the dining hall. This was meant to defang the strike enthusiasm of the students, given that they could no longer access food from the dining hall. But the strike leaders were determined. The strike took place during *zhezha* (a time of the year when crops in the fields have ripened). The leaders of the strike asked villagers from Mafala to bring ox drawn carts with cooked mealies for the borders to buy and eat. Business was brisk for the villagers. They could not help but smile at the windfall. The tooting horns of haulage trucks along the road that goes past Dadaya was replaced by the cracking of whips as villagers momentarily made the road theirs as they transported supplies of food for the borders with their donkey and ox-drawn carts.

Memories of the liberation struggle did not escape the ring leaders of the strike. They set up a committee, whose responsibility was to deal with *vatengesi* (counter-revolutionaries). This committee was akin to the Revolutionary tribunal set-up by Maximillian Robespierre during the French Revolution of the 18th century. Counter-revolutionaries were students who were accused of spying for the school authorities. They were accused of *mhosva dzinotsika* (crimes). I cannot remember the punishment meted on the *vatengesi*, but these were anxious moments for students who found themselves on the receiving end of the committee. Hell hath no fury like a "revolutionary tribunal" scoffed. The leaders of the strike instituted their own version of the "reign of terror". We followed their instructions like sheep being taken to the altar.

For four days, the strike leaders stood resolutely. They did not yield to pressure from school authorities to call off the strike. On day five, however, cracks began to emerge among the students. Most of the students had, had enough of the food supplies by villagers from Mafala. The students were missing food prepared at the dining hall. Others were sick and tired of the "reign of terror". Most of the students thought that the strike leaders had side-tracked and were no longer following the roadmap of the strike. How could the whole school be held to ransom by the lynch mob, the striking students wondered? One by one, students began to abandon the strike. The revolutionary fervour had fizzled out. On the sixth day, students resolved to go back to their classrooms and resume lessons. The strike was finally over much to the disappointment of the lynch mob.

Ringleaders, including the Ndege brothers and Sluza were punished severely. They weeded the school fields at "Siberia". They were also made to dig deep pits for close to two weeks.

Sluza remained unbroken. She called for more acts of defiance but her comrades in crime wanted to lie low as they plotted their next move. After two weeks, the strike ringleaders finished their punishment and joined others in their respective classes.

Chitanda meanwhile continued to bully other students. Chitanda, pencil slim and tall, was well known for unleashing a powerful left jab. He was feared by all and sundry. Some students attributed his fighting prowess to *mangoromera* (strength enhancing charm). His bullying was legendry. Many of the students beaten by Chitanda would not report him to the headmaster for fear of victimisation. Class monitors did not write down his name for noise making, they feared for their lives. Brain wise, he proved to be hermitically sealed. He more than compensated his lack of brains with his fighting power. He literally terrorised other students. Alcaeda would have looked at him with envy. The school authorities got wind of his bullying and Chitanda was expelled. That marked the end of a sad chapter at the mission school. Chitanda was declared *persona non grata* at Dadaya. Meanwhile, the Ndege brothers continued with their mischief.

The Ndege brothers' last hurrah was on the eve of their departure from Dadaya when they were left with one paper to finish their Ordinary Level examinations. They stole six chickens from the school fowl run. Instead of cooking the chickens away from the school premises, they cooked them in front of their dormitory. As junior students we could not understand how the Ndege brothers would give the game away in such a manner. Inevitably, they were caught by the boarding master after a tip-off from one of the prefects. The boarding master hid behind a tree and watched them like a leashed bulldog at a rabbit gambolling before it. He then charged at them. The chicken thieves could not run away. They were drunk and could only stagger. They were taken to the headmaster the following day. Resultantly, they were expelled from school before they had finished their examinations. Infantile delusion had gotten the better of the Ndege brothers.

Phew! What a time it was to be in boarding school – action packed, lots of fun, never short of drama - in short, these were events for the archives. The Ndege brothers and those of their ilk made headlines by entertaining us through their antics. Tragically, they paid heavily for their antics as they were unable to finish their education. Theirs was a lost chance, they were mischief makers, and they were a basket of deplorables.

7
The smooth operator

As a young boy growing up in the village in rural Zimbabwe, I had great admiration for Ronnie, the eternal teenager. Ronnie drove the latest cars. He also built a beautiful house in the village. I do not know how he made his fortune. I did not care. My friends and I would argue about how fast his car was. He drove a Peugeot 404 station wagon. For us, the Peugeot 404 station wagon was our ultimate dream car. We would ask our elder cousins to inscribe the name "Peugeot 404" on our toy cars, mostly made of disused bricks. All this was testimony to how much we revered Ronnie. Each time my friends and I saw Ronnie driving his Peugeot, we would break into a popular song back then, about a man who was run over by a Peugeot. The lyrics were:

> *Mumwe murume achienda kuguta*
> As a man was going to a city
> *Kunonditengera bheri-bheri bottom*
> To buy me a pair of bell bottoms
> *Pakudzoka akatsikwa nemota*
> When coming back, he was run over by a car
> *Mota yacho ndiyo piyo Peogeot*
> The car was a Peugeot

This was the era when bell bottoms where in fashion. Most young adults wore bell bottoms. I remember the first time I saw one of my cousin sisters who had been overseas, she was wearing a pair of bell bottoms. She brought business in the village to a halt as villagers scrambled to catch a glimpse of her.

Ronnie not to be outdone by other fashion-conscious villagers, was a proud owner of several pairs of bell bottoms. One's wardrobe would be incomplete without a *bheri* as the pair of bell bottoms was affectionately named in the village.

As we became older, we heard stories of Ronnie's shenanigans. Ronnie was rumoured to have stolen money from his white employers in the then Salisbury now Harare. He is said to have used his loot to buy cars. Some of the money was used to build his house, arguably the most beautiful in the village. How he escaped jail is a subject of debate. However, it was generally thought that he had an uncle who was a traditional healer. The uncle earned himself notoriety by using his charms to defend people caught on the wrong side of the law. Whether the charms worked or not was subject to speculation. For Ronnie, the charms worked.

Ronnie was a nickname; his real name was Madison Gwenhamo. He was nicknamed Ronnie after the notorious Ronnie Biggs, one of the thieves in the Great Train Robbery in Britain in 1964. Over the years, people forgot the name Madison, and everyone began calling him Ronnie. He appeared to like the nickname because he had the name Ronnie inscribed on his Peugeot 404. His Peugeot stood from the crowd. He attached feathers of the fish eagle to the aerial of his car radio, because he was of the *shiri* (bird) totem. Specifically, he was of the *Hungwe* (fish eagle) totem. Tied to the car grill, were claws which appeared to be of a leopard. The mats on the floor of the car also appeared to be leopard skins. At times he was heard "speaking" to the leopard skins. Some people thought that he had lost his marbles. To us, his fiercely loyal admirers, Ronnie was simply asserting his authority over the "leopard". He was our hero.

I had just read Charles Dickens' *Oliver Twist* that my father had bought for me. In the book was the character Jack Dawkins nicknamed the "Artful Dodger". For a while I thought the nickname would best suit Ronnie. I momentarily referred to him as the "Artful Dodger". This was after Ronnie's nephew walked me through some of his uncle's escapades. One of the tales was the allegation that during his time in prison he damaged his cell so badly that it needed repairs. Disguised as a handyman, he escaped. I then suggested that the nickname "Artful Dodger" was best suited for Ronnie. The nickname "Artful Dodger" could not make headway. My efforts were like a man whistling in the wind. The nickname Ronnie stuck.

He was also a gambler. One would think that when Kenny Rogers wrote the lyrics to his song, *The Gambler*, he had Ronnie in mind. Ronnie was streetwise. He knew when to walk away and when to run. Ronnie also took to heart that a gambler counts his money when the deal is done. On one occasion, Ronnie was involved in a bet with a wealthy businessman at the local business centre. The businessman owned a Mercedes Benz C-Class. The bet was about the outcome of a soccer match between two of the country's fiercest rivals – Dynamos and Highlanders. Ronnie was a staunch Dynamos supporter while the businessman supported Highlanders. If Dynamos won, Ronnie would walk away with the Mercedes Benz and a win for Highlanders meant Ronnie would lose his most prized possession, the Peugeot. Dynamos won the match thereby winning the Mercedes Benz for Ronnie. On that day, we were subjected to the unrelenting tooting horn of Ronnie's new acquisition, the Mercedes Benz. In retrospect, the Mercedes Benz was a ramshackle car, only that we were so excited about Ronnie's new acquisition to notice. I was one of the few lucky ones who happened to be offered a joyride by Ronnie. It was an honour to be offered a free ride in the village. The few occasions we were offered a ride was when the local *MuVhangeri* (evangelist) took his daughter to boarding school.

Ronnie was a speedy driver. I felt a surge of adrenaline when the car roared into life. However, the excitement of a ride in a Mercedes Benz got the better of me. I was all smiles despite the bumpy ride. I had faith in his driving abilities, after all he was my hero. Ronnie and the *MuVhangeri* were the only people who owned cars in the village. No wonder therefore, that Ronnie was immortalised by boys of my age.

Ronnie grew up in Harare's township of Highfield where his father was a cook at a local hotel. In Highfield, he did his primary education up to Grade Six. Ronnie never excelled in his school work and decided to abandon his education career prematurely. Life as a school drop-out was not rosy for Ronnie. He could not get a job. To survive, Ronnie would steal his parents' household goods. This did not go down well with his parents. After several efforts at trying to rehabilitate Ronnie, his parents decided to expel him from home. Homeless, and living the life of a vagabond, Ronnie slept in drainage pipes. He often ate food he found in bins.

With time, Ronnie met a gangster named Jack. Jack was a member of a gang that terrorised residents of the African townships of the then Harare, now Mbare, Highfield, and Kambuzuma. Ronnie was more than happy to join the gang. The gang was also involved in inter-party violence that is said to have erupted between the Zimbabwe African National Union (ZANU) and Zimbabwe African People's Union (ZAPU) in the 1960s. ZANU was a breakaway group from ZAPU. This resulted in internecine violence between the two parties. These were days of the rise of mass nationalism in the then Rhodesia. Ronnie and his gang took advantage of the violence to steal from residents of Highfield and Harare.

Always a step ahead of the police, Ronnie soon earned himself the smooth operator tag. He played his cards well. As young boys we were told of many episodes by Ronnie, the stuff of legends. Whether these stories were true or not, remained a guessing game. One of his episodes worthy of an Oscar was when Ronnie is said to have brought home a white woman as his wife to the village. During the colonial era, it was unheard of for a black man to marry a white woman. According to the legend, two neighbouring white commercial farmers were always at each's throats because one of the farmers had lost about 20 head of cattle to cattle rustlers. Rumours had it that the cattle had been stolen by the other farmer with the connivance of Ronnie.

Ronnie was a legendary playboy. In no time Ronnie started dating the farmer's daughter. The farmer was appalled that her daughter was dating a black man. He made all sorts of threats to Ronnie. Ronnie was not perturbed at all with these threats and even went to the extent of taking his newly found love to the village. A white person in the village was a rare sighting. That Ronnie had brought a white woman to the village made him a cult hero. This was headline news and soon the story spread. People descended on the village to catch a glimpse of Ronnie's *murungu* (white person). Those who felt that they were at peace with the English Language, would say to her, "Good morning madam", regardless of the time of the day. Others who knew their limitations with the English Language would only smile. Ronnie was eulogised. He had no reason to succumb to the incessant pressure from his new "father-in-law" by letting his newly found love go. He dug in.

Ronnie was a true believer in the wisdom of the ancient. In the village before you start digging for mice, you first identify and secure the mice's *mbudhlo* (escape route). You then close the *mbudhlo* and the mice are trapped and have nowhere to go. This means therefore that Ronnie had the farmer on leash, he could not do anything to Ronnie because he feared that Ronnie would report him to the police about the stolen cattle. The farmer was in a fix. The best the farmer could do was sulk about it. According to Ronnie's contemporaries however, the marriage to the white woman was short lived because after about two years she decided to go overseas to further her education. This did not change the new status of Ronnie in the village. After all, he had made history by bringing a *murungu* to the village. Ronnie moved on with his life.

He had an unquenchable thirst for immortality and would drink a concoction of herbs in the hope that he would remain young. He would sip his elixir of life with the aplomb of a *goremucheche* (eternal youth). He always shaved the little hair he had on his head so as to disguise his receding hairline.

Today Ronnie lives alone. Now an ageing Pollyanna, clearly, he can no longer cheat the ravages of old age. Ronnie is hardly seen outside his hut. Passers-by, stop near his home as if to pay homage to the once seemingly invincible smooth operator. They talk about his heyday. But Ronnie has moved from invincible to invisible.

8
The "Big Three" at Hweshoko

Holiday time in the village is about "who is who". Returnees, people coming back to the village mostly from the diaspora, try as much as they can to outclass each other in terms of possessions. Diasporans normally team up when they come back to the village. A cacophony of tooting horns announces their arrival. Whistling and ululating head for a crescendo as villagers welcome their famous sons and daughters from the diaspora. Celebrations are immediately set in motion with car stereos blaring loud music until late into the night as part of the rituals of hospitality. Denizens of the village also join in the fun. They flex their muscles by playing their stereos at full blast as if to tell the new arrivals that they also have radios. The village erupts into life.

Diasporans are revered in the village. This has not been lost to the diasporans as they flaunt their new found "wealth" for all to see. They buy expensive cars. The local shopping centre becomes an arena for fierce competition. The diasporans park their cars at strategic positions where they are seen by passers-by. They buy beer and drink it while standing within close proximity to their cars, just in case some people might doubt their ownership of the cars. They make use of errand boys and girls from the village who are more than happy to do chores for the diasporans. Doing errands comes with "benefits". The errand boys and girls who are mostly unemployed, are given a few dollars for their pains. Also, doing errands means "free" beer for the errand boys and girls. This is the time of the year when the errand boys and girls drink imported lagers such as Heineken, Windhoek Lager, and Amstel, courtesy of the diasporans.

The diasporans from England bring soccer jerseys of their favourite teams such as Arsenal, Manchester United, Liverpool, Chelsea and those from South Africa bring rugby jerseys of the *Amabokoboko*, the rugby team and *Bafana-bafana*, the soccer team. Those who want to show-off that they have scaled the academic ladder bring t-shirts labelled the names of their former universities. The t-shirts are written on them names of such revered institutions as the University of Cape Town, Rhodes University, Oxford University, Stanford University, University of Melbourne, and the University of British Columbia. Villagers wearing soccer jerseys of European soccer teams are a common sight in the village.

Rumours fly thick and fast about the source of the wealth of the diasporans and a few locals who have made it against all odds. Some of the villages have their fair share of diasporans and a few locals living large. Hweshoko village has its fair share of notables. Among the "who is who" in Hweshoko, inevitably are a MuDealer (wheeler dealer) named Jonah Devera, popularly known as JD, Sponono an *injiva* based in South Africa and Ndaiziveyi a career civil servant whose new found wealth has been a subject of contestation. In the village of Hweshoko, these three men commanded respect among the villagers because of their upward mobility on the social ladder.

Sponono is said to have gone to South Africa at a tender age of 17 after doing Form Four. His Form Four results are a subject of speculation. No one really knows if he passed or not. Sponono joined the "Great Trek" to Johannesburg to look for a job. The practice of seeking employment in Johannesburg by Zimbabweans dates back to the colonial era. Back in the day, men left their homes to seek a fortune in South Africa as migrant labourers. They mostly travelled by foot. Some were not as lucky as they were killed by wild animals. Those who made it worked on the gold and diamond mines in Johannesburg. They came back to be welcomed as heroes. An individual who had gone to work in Johannesburg was nicknamed *Mujubheki* after the name Johannesburg. *Mujubheki* dressed very well. The whole village was in awe of *Mujubheki*. An unmarried *Mujubheki* was the most eligible bachelor in the village. Would-be brides fell over each other in a bid to impress *Mujubheki*. A *Mujubheki's* residence came to be known as *pamusha paMujubheki* (Mujubheki's home). Some *Mujubhekis* would live in Johannesburg for as many as 15 years without going back home. In the village, such an individual was called *Muchoni* (the forgotten one). When he finally came back home (at times with a family in trail), there were huge festivities in the village to celebrate *Muchoni's* homecoming. Thus, it was not rare for *Muchoni* to marry a South African woman. Relatives would be at pains to try and teach the new bride the local language and customs.

Today, is the latter-day *Mujubheki*, as encapsulated by Sponono the *injiva*. When Sponono went to Johannesburg, people in the village did not hear about him for close to ten years. Some thought he had been murdered, others said he had married a local South African woman who did not want him to go back to Zimbabwe. However, Sponono decided to go back home for a visit. And lo and behold, he was accompanied by a wife, a white woman from South Africa, and two daughters. The village was "humming, electric" with the news of the *murungu* brought by Sponono. Sponono's father could not believe that his son had married a white woman. He was all smiles and was even surprised further that his white daughter-in-law could speak a few words in Shona. The daughter-in-law reassured her new relatives that she had no qualms with eating African traditional dishes. She even mentioned by name a few dishes eaten in the village. Many in the village laughed because of the way Sponono's wife pronounced Shona words. Village jesters joined in the fun. They pronounced Shona words the way the *murungu* did, leaving villagers in stitches.

There were celebrations in the village to welcome the white *muroora* (daughter-in-law). Sponono's relatives brought presents to welcome his new family. Sponono's parents slaughtered a cow as a way of showing happiness for their *muroora*. Friends and relatives descended on the village. They all wanted to take selfies with the *murungu*. As per dictates of the village, the *muroora* wore a *dook* (head dress) and a long dress and wrapped a *zambia* (piece of cloth) round her waist. Speaker after speaker gave their blessings to the couple. One of Sponono's sisters sat close to the *muroora* whispering into the *muroora*'s ear (English words) so that the *muroora* would keep abreast with the proceedings. Some of the *tetes* (aunties) spoke in English, though broken, they nevertheless provided entertainment to the crowd. The English they spoke is what is known in the village as *Shonglish* (a combination of Shona and English). Clearly, the aunties were trying to impress the *murungu*. Most of the speakers showed their happiness that Sponono had brought a white *muroora* to the village. However, Sponono's grandmother could not hide her disgust at Sponono for bringing a *murungu* home. She said that she wanted Sponono to marry in the village. She went further to mention the name of the prospective bride. Her thoughts were premised on a Shona proverb, *rooranayi vematongo* (marry from your neighbourhood). This was a practice from the old days. A son was encouraged to marry from the neighbourhood. This thinking was based on the idea that the families of the new couple new each other and if any differences arose between the husband and wife, they would be solved amicably by the elders of the two families. This would ensure the survival of the marriage.

Meanwhile, it was all smiles for the *muroora*. She greatly appreciated the presents she had been showered with. The presents included about 20 chickens "without borders" (free-range chickens), three goats and a cow. Women brought the *muroora*, a *rusero* (willowing basket), and lots of utensils. The *muroora* was given a chance to speak. The only Shona word she spoke was, "*Makadhini?*" (How are you?). Of course, she had challenges in pronouncing the Shona words correctly. After her speech, the crowd broke into song to show their happiness. They whistled and ululated. Their happiness realised no bounds.

Sponono came home driving his sleek Mercedes Benz E class, the ultimate status symbol. His parents were on cloud nine. They told everyone who cared to listen about Sponono's car, a rare sight in the village. The parents also showed their relatives, clothes that Sponono had bought them from South Africa. For the parents, seeing Sponono and their white *muroora* standing next to their Mercedes Benz in the heart of the village, was something akin to a surreal Disney scene.

One other notable in the village is Kefas, a *mudealer* (wheeler-dealer). A dealer in the villager is a person who is involved in shady deals in order to make money. Dealers therefore, reside in the underworld. Kefas made a huge fortune out of fleecing *makorokoza*, (illegal gold miners).

The other notable was Ndayiziveyi, a high ranking civil servant. He was good in class and wrote for himself a small piece of history starting from the days he was in junior school.

For his secondary education, Ndaiziveyi went to Thornhill High School, about 260 km to the south of Harare. At Thornhill High School, he excelled especially in the Arts subjects. He always got prizes in History and Geography. He was not bad in the sciences either.

At a time when some of his schoolmates were engaging in many vices such as drinking beer and taking drugs, Ndayiziveyi shunned such bad habits. He has remained a teetotaller to this day. However, during his days as an "A" (Advanced) Level, Ndaiziveyi caught the eye of a beauty named Ruvarashe. Ruva, as Ndaiziveyi affectionately called her, was a year his junior at Thornhill High School. Ruva was also a village girl from Gomututu in the district of Zvishavane. She had made a name for herself as an extremely talented tennis player. She had endeared herself to the hearts of many. These were the years when Zimbabwe had just gained independence in the 1980s. Thornhill was a former school for white students. With the advent of independence, blacks enrolled at the former white schools. Racism was evident at these former white schools. Sports disciplines such as rugby, hockey, and tennis were the preserve of whites. Ruva was the odd person out in the school tennis team. She would at times, be subjected to racial insults from some white members of the team. Ruva would seek solace from her shoulder to cry on, her boyfriend Ndayiziveyi.

In class, Ruva proved to be equally gifted. She won several academic awards. When she was in the last year of her "A" Level, she was elected head girl of her school. Meanwhile Ndayiziveyi had enrolled for a Social Anthropology degree at the University of Zimbabwe. But the two lovebirds continued with their love affair. These were the days of letter writing. The mention of mobile phones would have attracted scorn and revulsion. No one would have envisioned that the technological juggernaut would usher the mobile phones a few years later. Thus, Ndayiziveyi and Ruva were content to communicate through letters and on a few occasions, they used a public phone to communicate.

As the saying goes, out of site out of mind. With time, Ndayiziveyi fell in a love with Chipo, also a first year student at the University of Zimbabwe. It seemed he had called time on his relationship with Ruva who was still in Gweru completing her "A" Level. Ruva got wind of this new development and sought permission from the school authorities to visit Harare, ostensibly to visit a doctor. The moment she got to the university, all hell broke loose. She made a beeline to Chipo's room at Carr-Saunders Hall of residence. She found Chipo in her room and immediately a fight broke out. That she was an athlete meant that Ruva was as fit as a fiddle. She made mincemeat of Chipo. The fight was over in no time.

The victorious Ruva then went to Ndayiziveyi's hall of residence. Ndayiziveyi was not in the room. Ndayiziveyi had become part of the furniture at the student union bar. If he was not with Chipo, he was with his drinking partners Dzvatswatswa, Mafaro and Muparaz. They were well-known for their love of alcohol. Nicknamed, "The Four Brothers" after a popular musical group based in Harare, they formed an acapella group. They entertained other patrons at the student union bar.

Ruva meanwhile had found Naiyeziveyi's door closed. Ndayiziveyi's neighbour advised her to look for him at the student union bar. She found Ndayiziveyi in a drunken stupor. Ndayiziveyi was dragged kicking and screaming to his room by Ruva. Ruva left Ndayiziveyi and went to sleep with a friend at Swinton. The following day Ndayiziveyi pleaded for forgiveness from Ruva. This was uncharacteristic of Ndayiziveyi, a very proud man, who claimed to know everything from the ocean floor to the sky. It took the intervention of Ruva's friend for the two to reconcile. Within a year Ruva also enrolled at the University of Zimbabwe. After their education, Ndayiziveyi and Ruva married and decided to settle in Harare. They enjoyed unalloyed bliss. Ndayiziveyi was appointed an officer in the public service and rose through the ranks to become a director. Ruva got a job as a teacher at a high school in Harare.

Ndayiziveyi got meagre pickings from his job in the civil service. He found the going tough. But his lifestyle began to change. He bought a beautiful car, a BMW 5 series model. His salary did not match the car he was driving. Tongues were wagging about the source of his income. People would ask him questions about his found new status. Sometimes he would smile and happily answer questions about his nouvou riche status. At times he would give a cold shoulder. Understandingly so. Although he led a simple life, it appeared corruption had rubbed onto him. His lifestyle did not justify his salary. He bought a house in Borrowdale, a leafy suburb of Harare. Rumours had to it that he also owned several houses in Bulawayo, the second largest city in Zimbabwe.

Another character in Hweshoko village was, *Mu*Dealer, a high school dropout. His real name was Kefas. Kefas was born to a family of seven, one girl and six boys. Their parents were not well-off. They did not own cattle. The only livestock they had were three goats. The numbers of the goats never rose because the parents kept selling them each time they increased so as to raise school fees for their children. Kefas and his siblings did not do justice to the parents' efforts at trying to educate them. The children's performance in class ranged from average to well below average.

Kefas did his primary education at the local school Hwida. After his primary education he went to Rusununguko Secondary School, about 10km away. Kefas was a complete stranger to high grades. He would either be the last in his class or the second last. At times he would dodge class and hide in the Hweshoko hills until others had finished school. His parents tried everything in their power to rectify the situation but all was in vain. Kefas eventually dropped from school when he had started his Form Four.

Kefas went to look for a job in the nearby town of Shurugwi. He found a job as a gardener. As a gardener, Kefas earned a meagre salary. He supplemented his salary by moonlighting for a local security company. Most of his money was spent recklessly at the town's two nightclubs. His love for women and alcohol was unparalleled. He hardly visited his parents in the village. Kefas remained in Shurugwi town for the next ten years during which he made a name for himself, albeit for the wrong reasons.

Shurugwi town is within proximity to small gold mines mostly abandoned where many youths try their luck at mining. The gold mining was mostly illegal. These gold miners are called *makorokoza*. The *makorokoza* are governed by the law of the jungle. Many have lost their lives because of the many scuffles that take place in the underworld of the *makorokoza*. However, some of the *makorokoza*, through unscrupulous practices have made a fortune for themselves. This spurred Kefas to try his luck as a *mukorokoza*.

He quit his job in a huff and joined other *makorokoza* in 'jungle'. Kefas soon realised that being a *korokoza* was not a bed of roses. He was roughed-up by other *makorokoza*. Kefas' cowardice is the stuff of legends. Growing-up in the village with other boys of his age, Kefas was the favourite punching bag (both literally and metaphorically). He never lasted a minute in a fight. He was a mere grasshopper, an ineffectual blowhard, who would collapse at the first sign of gunfire. Boys' fights were a form of entertainment in the village. Kefas had to learn survival tactics if he was to make headway in his new "venture".

There in the rough, hostile, and unforgiving environment of the underworld, Kefas mastered the ropes of the trade. He graduated from the "university of hard knocks". There in the tunnels of the disused mines, he learned things about life that one cannot learn in a university lecture room. His transformation was rapid. He had moved from the coward of the village to the bully of the "tunnel". Kefas began to make "big money".

Back in the village, rumours spread about Kefas' rags to riches story. In no time Kefas bought a Toyota Prado SUV. He built a beautiful house for his parents and even bought them a car. Kefas also bought several houses in Gweru, about 60 km to the north west of Shurugwi. In the village, Kefas earned himself the nickname *Mu*Dealer. Nicknames are sticky in the village. The majority of the people were now calling him *Mu*Dealer. *Mu*Dealer was no longer confined to Shurugwi alone, he would go anywhere in the country where the "gold rush" took him. He had become part of a gang called *Ma*Shurugwi" (gold dealers from Shurugwi). *Ma*Shurugwi were notorious for their violence. The *Ma*Shurugwi are said to originate from Shurugwi where they cut their *chikorokoza* teeth in disused gold mines. This, however, appears to be incorrect as the so-called *Ma*shurugwi are in essence a motley crew of *makorokoza* from Shurugwi and other parts of the country.

Meanwhile *Mu*Dealer had unbridled political ambitions and would one day want to represent his constituency as a local Member of Parliament, he has started doling out food handouts to the elderly and infirm. He also has started projects for the youths. These include chicken farming and goat revolving projects. Resultantly, *Mu*Dealer has assembled a group of youths who act as his storm troopers. They are fiercely loyal to *Mu*Dealer, and are prepared to defend him at any cost. This has given *Mu*Dealer a sense of security. He sees politics as the only viable route to safeguard his newly acquired empire. *Mu*Dealer, a poster child of obscene wealth, subsequently got elected as a member of parliament in his home area.

Thus, the stage for a struggle for supremacy in the village had been set in motion featuring the "Big Three". MuDealer, Sponono, the *injiva*, and Ndayiziveyi. The "Big Three" were all in an undeclared competition about who was the most successful. In the village the fetishisation of money has led people to universalise the definition of success in material terms. The "Big Three" are poster boys of this fetishisation of money.

Glossary

Bheri	a pair of bell bottoms
Chembere	the elderly
Dube	of the zebra totem
Injiva	Zimbabwean migrant workers in South Africa
Gidha mangauzane	run storks
Goremucheche	eternal youth
Hayibo	to refuse
Humwe	work party
Hurudza	accomplished farmer/farmers
Kudenga hakuna roya	heaven has no lawyer
Kumakomba	pits for torturing suspected war collaborators
Kandiro kanopfumba kunobva kamwe	one good turn deserves another
Magonyeti	haulage trucks
Mangoromera	strength enhancing charm
Mbuya	grandmother
Muchoni	the forgotten one
MuVhangeri	evangelist
Mudealer	someone involved in shady deals
Mujubheki	someone who worked in Johannesburg
Muroora	daughter-in-law
Ndari	village pubs
Ruzhowa	a 'fence' made of thorny branches
Rusero	willowing basket
Sadza	maize meal thick porridge

Sekuru	grandfather
Shona	the dominant language/race in Zimbabwe
Shonglish	a combination of Shona and English
Sidudhla	obese woman
Tete	aunt
Tsvimbodzemoto	firearms
VaChorara	Mr Chorara
Vahosi	senior wife in a polygynous marriage
Vakomana	boys (liberation fighters)
Vasikana	girls (liberation fighters)
VaVhangeri	evangelists
Yhuuu	to be surprised

Printed in the United States
By Bookmasters